Katie Woo's
* Neighborhood *

PICTURE WINDOW BOOKS
a capstone imprint

Katie Woo's Neighborhood is published by Picture Window Books,
a Capstone imprint
1710 Roe Crest Drive
North Mankato, Minnesota 56003
www.capstonepub.com

Cataloging-in-Publication Data is available on the
Library of Congress website.
ISBN: 978-1-5158-4668-0

Summary: Katie Woo loves her community. But it's not just the parks,
stores, and services that make the neighborhood great—it's the all of
the people who build the community and make it work. With every
new neighbor Katie meets, she's inspired to find new ways to be an
awesome neighbor herself!

Graphic Designer: Bobbie Nuytten

Printed and bound in the USA.
PA70

Table of Contents

Katie's Neighborhood

Police

Library

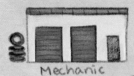
Mechanic

City
Hall

Grocery Store

Post Office

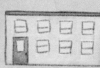

Helping Mayor Patty

Katie told Pedro and JoJo,

"We have a new neighbor!"

They ran to meet her.

"Hi!" said the girl. "My

name is Haley O'Hara."

"Cool name," said Katie.

"I have five brothers and sisters," Haley bragged.

"We have enough players for a soccer team," said Katie.

"Let's do it!" yelled Haley. "My brothers and sisters are already playing."

Katie's mom told her,
"You can play later. Today
is Aunt Patty's first town
meeting as our new mayor.
Let's go wish her luck."

At City Hall, Mayor Patty said, "Today our city council will decide how to spend our tax money."

Katie smiled. "I love money."

"First let's begin by talking about what each neighborhood needs the most," said Aunt Patty. "Then the council will vote."

"My neighborhood is growing," said Mr. Mann. "We need a fire station."

Pedro told Katie, "Our neighborhood needs ice cream."

"Our streetlights are not bright," said Ms. Miller. "We need better ones."

"My streetlight is fine," Katie told JoJo. "I can sit by my window and read."

"I wonder what our neighborhood needs," Katie said to her friends. "I will draw a picture of our block. It will help me think."

Mr. Davis raised his
hand and said, "Please
send someone to stop pesky
squirrels from eating all my
bird food."

Mayor Patty told Mr. Davis, "I'm sorry. Our town can't fix that."

"I'll help you," said Pedro's mom. "I'll show you a better bird feeder."

An angry man said, "We need more garbage cans. Our blocks are stinky."

"Pew!" Katie laughed. "I'm glad our block is not stinky."

Katie told JoJo, "Look at my picture. What is missing from our block?"

"How about puppies in every yard?" said JoJo.

"Puppies would be fun!"

said Katie. "But not necessary."

"On hot days," said Pedro,

"ice cream is necessary."

"Let's think," said JoJo.
"What did we see on our
way here?"

"I saw kids playing in the
street," said Pedro. "A lot of
them!"

"That's it!" said Katie.

"Playing in the street is

dangerous. I know what our

neighborhood needs: a park!"

"A park for baseball!"

said JoJo.

"And soccer!" said Pedro.

"And sledding!" shouted

Katie.

Katie raised her hand. "In our neighborhood, kids are playing in the street. We need a park."

"Let's vote on it!" said Mayor Patty.

The council began to

vote. They voted to spend

money on a new fire station,

better lights, more garbage

cans, and . . . a park!

On the way home, Katie told Haley O'Hara, "Soon there will be a big surprise for you! Your brothers and sisters will like it too."

They did!

Stocking Up for the Storm

Katie was watching TV.

"A storm is coming," said
the weather lady. "A big one!"

"Wowzee!" yelled Katie.

"The storm may last for days," said Katie's dad. "We need lots of food."

Katie agreed. "Lots of cookies!"

Katie's mom made a list.

"We need milk and cheese and meat and fruit."

"And cookies," reminded Katie.

The grocery store was crowded. Katie said hi to JoJo and Pedro.

"Don't worry," Mr. Nelson told Katie. "I've stocked up on everything."

Katie found the milk in the dairy section. She found chicken in the meat section.

"Good work, Katie!" said her dad.

Katie told her mom, "We need tomato soup too. If the storm is scary, tomato soup will cheer me up."

"Cookies and ice cream cheer me up too," said Katie. "Let's get both. Dad has a credit card, so we don't have to pay."

"I do have to pay," said

Katie's dad. "I must pay when

I get the credit card bill."

"Oh," said Katie.

"These cookies are on sale,"

said Katie. "Can we get them?"

"Yes," said her mom.

"Smart shopper!"

Haley O'Hara and her five

brothers and sisters ran into

the store. They bumped into a

tower of toilet paper.

CRASH!

"Wow!" shouted Haley. "I'm glad it wasn't grape juice. Let's pile it up again."

"Cool!" said Katie. "It's like making a snowman."

Miss Winkle came in.

She told Katie, "I need food for my new puppy. His name is Twinkle."

Katie smiled. "He rhymes with you."

"Twinkle hates storms," said Miss Winkle. "He hides under the bed."

"Oh," said Katie. "I hope I don't need to hide under the bed!"

Katie joined JoJo and Pedro at the checkout line.

"We got a lot of hot chocolate," said Pedro.

"I got spaghetti," said JoJo. "It's fun to eat!"

Back home, Katie watched

the wild wind shaking the trees.

She said, "I hope the birds'

nests don't fall down."

Katie decided, "I need
tomato soup and grilled
cheese for dinner. And a
cookie for dessert."

It all tasted great!

"I hope my friends are okay," said Katie. She called JoJo.

"I'm painting. You should see the storm I made," said JoJo. "It's fierce!"

Pedro was
loving his hot
chocolate.

Haley and
her wild brothers
and sisters were making
an angel food cake.

The storm went on for a long time. But everyone in Katie's neighborhood was safe and cozy.

Katie fell asleep with a
smile. She dreamed that
Mr. Nelson and his family
were cozy too.

And it was true!

Friends in the Mail

Katie made a scarf for her grandpa's birthday. It took her a long time.

"We should mail it today," said Katie's mom. "Grandpa's birthday is very soon."

"Let's go!" said Katie.

Katie and her mom began

walking to the post office.

"Hey, Katie," yelled Pedro.

"Look at the soccer stickers

I got in the mail."

"They look cool!" said Katie. "Maybe I'll order some too. But right now we have to mail my grandpa's present."

On the next block, Katie

saw Sharon, her mail carrier.

Sharon was telling JoJo, "I

have something for you."

"Look!" said JoJo. "I wrote a letter to an astronaut, and I got a photo back."

"Great!" said Sharon.

"I love bringing happy mail!"

Katie and her mom
hurried to the post office.
They saw trucks bringing
in mail and trucks taking
other mail away.

"Hi, Miss Roxie," Katie said to the clerk. "I want to mail this birthday present. I hope it gets there in time."

Miss Roxie smiled. "It will!

We deliver in sunny weather

and in the rain and the snow."

Just then, Haley O'Hara

and her five brothers and sisters

came into the post office.

"We are mailing letters
to our pen pals," said Haley.
"They all live in different cities."

Katie asked Miss Roxie,

"How do you know where

to send each letter?"

"With zip codes," said Miss Roxie. "That helps us sort each letter. Then it will go to the right place."

"Does the mail always travel in trucks?" asked Haley. "I want to be a truck driver when I grow up."

"No," said Miss Roxie.

"The mail also goes by plane

and sometimes by boat."

As Katie and her mom left the post office, Katie waved at a mail truck.

She said, "I hope they take good care of my grandpa's present."

On the way home, Katie's
mom asked, "Have you ever
heard about the Pony Express?"
"No," said Katie.

Her mother explained, "A long time ago, mail was carried from place to place on horses."

"Wow!" said Katie. "I'd love to be the rider and bring birthday presents."

When Katie got home,
she called her grandpa and
said, "I mailed you a present
for your birthday. I hope you
like it."

Katie's gift arrived in time.

Did her grandpa love it?

He did!

Super Paramedic!

Katie and her grandma
were having lunch.

"I love your new bracelet,"
said Katie.

"Me too!" said Grandma.
"Hearts are the best."

After lunch, Grandma

was ready to go home.

Katie said, "I'll walk you

to your car."

Whoosh! Haley O'Hara
came skating by with her
brothers and sisters.

"Hi!" yelled Katie.

"Hi!" yelled Haley.

Grandma told Katie,
"My car is at the end of
the block."

They had almost reached
the car, when—

Grandma tripped on a broken sidewalk!

She fell down—hard!

"I hurt my foot," said

Grandma. "I can't move it."

Katie wanted to cry, but

she stayed calm.

"I'll go get Mom," she said.

Katie's mom called 911.

She told Grandma, "The

paramedics will be here soon.

They will help you."

"I hope so," said Katie.

Haley O'Hara said, "Put my sweater on your grandma. She should keep warm until the ambulance comes."

"How do you know that?"

asked Katie.

"My family is always

breaking something," said

Haley. "I have lots of practice."

Soon they heard the loud siren. The paramedics were there!

Katie was so happy to see them.

One paramedic listened to
Grandma's heart.

The other one examined
Grandma's foot.

"Your heart is fine," said

one of the paramedics. "But

I think your ankle is broken.

We need to take you to the

hospital."

The paramedics lifted

Grandma into the ambulance.

They were gentle and strong.

Katie and her mom drove

to the hospital.

At the hospital, a doctor

put a cast on Grandma's foot.

She told her, "After six weeks

you will be fine."

Grandma smiled. "Thank
you! I want to thank the
paramedics too."

But they had rushed to
another accident.

Katie said, "Grandma,

I'm glad you will get better.

But I am sad that you lost

your new bracelet. It's gone!"

But it wasn't! When Katie

got home, Haley was waiting.

"Here is your grandma's

bracelet. I found it in the grass."

Katie hugged Haley. "You're

the best!"

Then she called Grandma.

"Haley found your bracelet!"

"Terrific!" said Grandma.

"There is one more thing
I want to do," said Katie.
She got out her paper
and paints.

Katie began to write and
draw.

"Hearts are the best,"
Katie said. She drew a lot
of them.

Dear Paramedics,
thank you so much
for helping my
grandma. You
are SUPER!

Love,
Katie

More About Mayors

Where they work: city hall

What they do: Mayors oversee the city's main departments like police, fire, schools, and transportation. They also hold and run city council meetings.

What they wear: Most of the time mayors wear dressy clothes.

More About Grocers

Where they work: grocery stores

What they do: Grocers run grocery stores. They order food and supplies and make sure it is displayed and available for customers to buy.

What they wear: Grocers wear nice clothes, a name tag, and sometimes an apron.

More About Mail Carriers

Where they work: outside and at the post office

What they do: Mail carriers deliver packages and letters to homes and businesses.

What they wear: Mail carriers where a uniform of dark blue pants or shorts and light blue shirts. They may also wear a hat and coat.

More About Paramedics

Where they work: an ambulance

What they do: Paramedics treat sick or injured people. They drive the patients to the hospital if needed.

What they wear: Paramedics wear uniforms consisting of pants, a shirt, and a name tag.

About the Author

Fran Manushkin is the author of Katie Woo, the highly acclaimed, fan-favorite early reader series, as well as the popular Pedro series. Her other books include *Happy in Our Skin*, *Baby, Come Out!* and the best-selling board books *Big Girl Panties* and *Big Boy Underpants*. There is a real Katie Woo: Fran's great-niece, who doesn't get into trouble like the Katie in the books. Fran lives in New York City, three blocks from Central Park, where she can often be found bird-watching and daydreaming. She writes at her dining room table, without the help of her two naughty cats, Chaim and Goldy.

About the Illustrator

Laura Zarrin spent her early childhood in the St. Louis, Missouri, area. There she explored creeks, woods, and attic closets, climbed trees, and dug for artifacts in the backyard, all in preparation for her future career as an archeologist. She never became one, however, because she realized she's much happier drawing in the comfort of her own home while watching TV. When she was twelve, her family moved to the Silicon Valley in California, where she still resides with her very logical husband and teen sons, and their illogical dog, Cody.